Kandu
FUN AND GAMES

written by:
Shannon Barnes

illustrated by:
Herb Moore

tate publishing
CHILDREN'S DIVISION

Published by Tate Publishing & Enterprises, LLC
127 E. Trade Center Terrace | Mustang, Oklahoma 73064 USA
1.888.361.9473 | www.tatepublishing.com

Book design copyright © 2016 by Tate Publishing, LLC. All rights reserved.
Cover and interior design by Eileen Cueno
Illustrations by Herb Moore

Published in the United States of America

ISBN: 978-1-68270-616-9
1. Juvenile Fiction / Animals / General
2. Juvenile Fiction / Stories In Verse
16.03.11

THIS BOOK BELONGS TO:

Hello there, friends, how do you do?

It's such a pleasure to meet you. My name is Kandu!

I live in the Arctic, where it's icy and cold.

We play games to stay warm, games new and old!

I'm growing up now, so I spend more time in school,

Where we learn new games and remember the rules!

Last year we swam in the water, racing polar bears and seals,

And we never needed slides as we slid down snowy hills.

I have so many stories and games that you should play.

The only rules are to have fun and never shy away.

As long as you're having fun, you can never really lose.

Take it from my brother, who once forgot the rules.

He stopped me when I came home from school one day

And gruffly asked me, "What did you play?"

I said, "Duck Duck Goose!" So my brother asked,

"Did you win? Did you win? Were you best in your class?"

"Oh yes, oh yes!" I said, smiling. "Yes, I won.

I got to go outside. It was so much fun!

I got to run and laugh. I got to skip and play.

I heard the birds sing to each other. Oh, how I won today!"

Then I came home from school another day,

And my brother grumbled, "What did you play?"

I said, "Ping-Pong!" And you know what he asked?

"Did you win? Did you win? Were you best in your class?"

I smiled so big and said, "Of course, I won!

I got to play with my friend. I got to have fun.

We paddled back and forth, but before the game was done,

We fell over laughing. Oh, how I won!"

My brother growled and said, "That's not what I mean.

When you win, you do better. You beat the other team!

You have the high score, and your friend's score is low.

Tell me if you win tomorrow. I will be proud, you know!"

I came home from school the next day,

And my brother asked me, "What did you play?"

I said, "Basketball." And I knew he would ask,

"Did you win? Did you win? Were you best in your class?"

I could just whisper, "No, I don't think so."

Jesse's score was high, and my score was low.

I cried because I lost, then hid my face with my hands.

"I don't know how to make you proud. I don't think I can."

My brother dropped his head and could feel he was wrong.

In his ears he could hear the words to our mom and dad's song.

They'd sing, "Winning doesn't mean your score's high or low.

It's learning to say, "I can!" Because trying is how we grow."

I said to my brother, "I'm sorry I didn't win."

"No, I'm sorry," he said with an understanding grin.

"You always say I can! That's why your name's Kandu!

You remembered to make life fun, and now I remember too."

e|LIVE

listen|imagine|view|experience

AUDIO BOOK DOWNLOAD INCLUDED WITH THIS BOOK!

In your hands you hold a complete digital entertainment package. In addition to the paper version, you receive a free download of the audio version of this book. Simply use the code listed below when visiting our website. Once downloaded to your computer, you can listen to the book through your computer's speakers, burn it to an audio CD or save the file to your portable music device (such as Apple's popular iPod) and listen on the go!

How to get your free audio book digital download:

1. Visit www.tatepublishing.com and click on the e|LIVE logo on the home page.
2. Enter the following coupon code:
   f63e-ceda-d76d-97fb-5b84-3e80-926d-bc0a
3. Download the audio book from your e|LIVE digital locker and begin enjoying your new digital entertainment package today!